The Story of Alexander Fleming

Alan Trussell-Cullen

The Story of Alexander Fleming

Fast Forward
Gold Level 22

Text: Alan Trussell-Cullen
Editor: Johanna Rohan
Design: Stella Vassiliou
Series design: James Lowe
Production controller: Seona Galbally
Photo research: Gillian Cardinal
Audio recordings: Juliet Hill, Picture Start
Spoken by: Matthew King and Abbe Holmes
Reprint: Jennifer Foo

Acknowledgements
The author and publisher would like to acknowledge permission to reproduce material from the following sources:
Photographs by Akg-images, pp 11, 20; Corbis Australia Pty Ltd, pp 6, 18 left, 22; Emerald City Images/Popperfoto, pp 7, 12, 23 top; Getty Images, pp 13, 15-6; Lonley Planet Images/Wayne Walton, p 23 bottom; Photolibrary, pp 1, 4-5, 8-10, 14, 17, 18 right; Science & Society Picture Library, p 21; Wellcome Library, London, p 19.

ISBN 978 0 17 012691 5
ISBN 978 0 17 012681 6 (set)

Cengage Learning Australia
Level 7, 80 Dorcas Street
South Melbourne, Victoria Australia 3205
Phone: 1300 790 853

Cengage Learning New Zealand
Unit 4B Rosedale Office Park
331 Rosedale Road, Albany, North Shore NZ 0632
Phone: 0800 449 725

For learning solutions, visit **cengage.com.au**

Printed in Australia by Ligare Pty Ltd
7 8 9 10 11 12 13 22 21 20 19 18

Evaluated in independent research by staff from the Department of Language, Literacy and Arts Education at the University of Melbourne.

The Story of Alexander Fleming

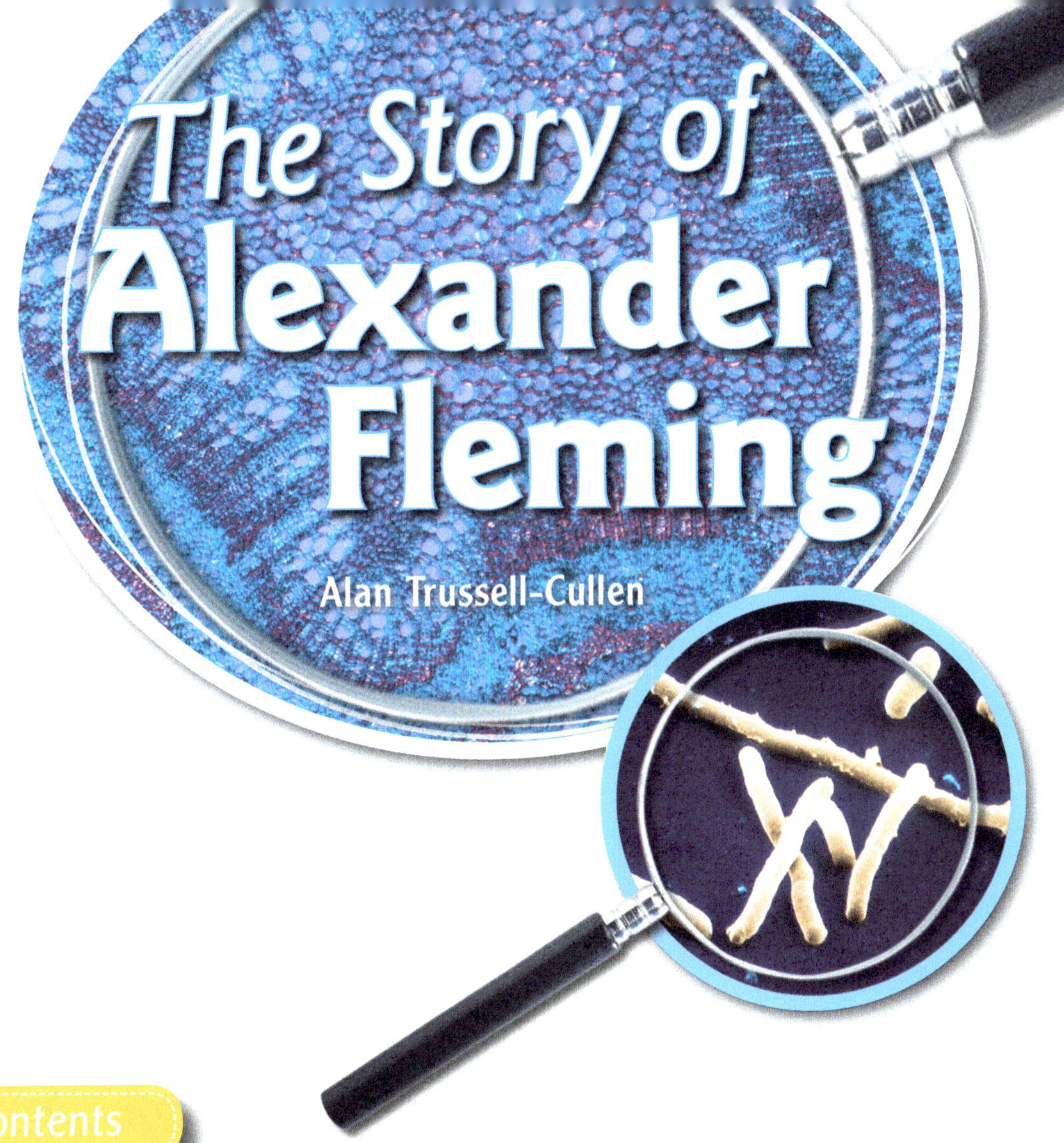

Alan Trussell-Cullen

Contents

Chapter 1

INTRODUCTION

Today, there are special medicines called antibiotics that help the body fight **bacteria**.
But, there was a time –
not that long ago –
when antibiotics didn't exist,
and many people died from **infections** caused by bacteria.

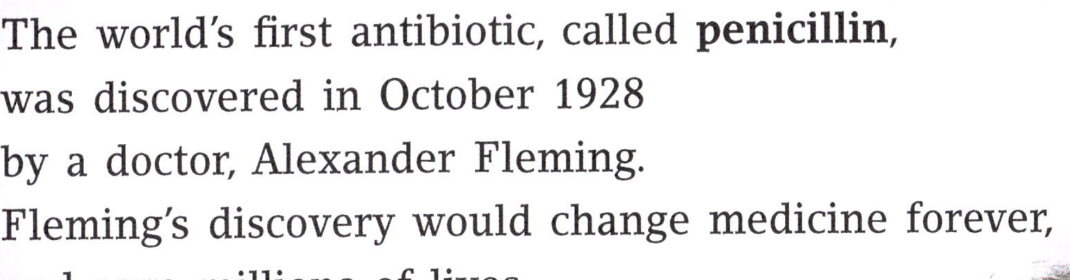

The world's first antibiotic, called **penicillin**, was discovered in October 1928 by a doctor, Alexander Fleming. Fleming's discovery would change medicine forever, and save millions of lives.

Bacteria can only be seen with a microscope. When they enter a wound, they can grow quickly from a few **cells** to millions of cells. The human body has ways of protecting itself from bacteria, but if there are too many bacteria, the person can become very sick and may even die.

Chapter 2

FLEMING'S EARLY LIFE

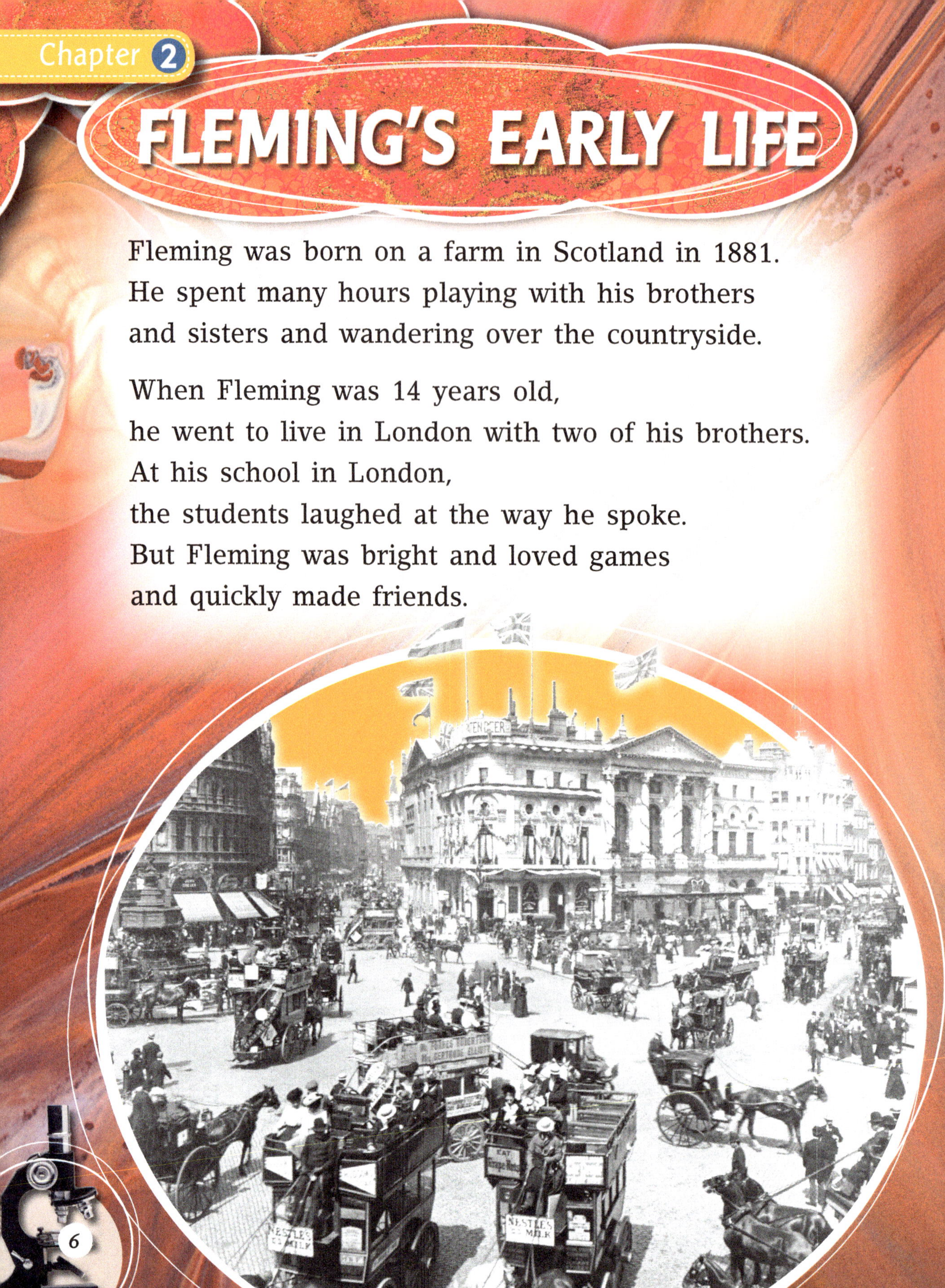

Fleming was born on a farm in Scotland in 1881. He spent many hours playing with his brothers and sisters and wandering over the countryside.

When Fleming was 14 years old, he went to live in London with two of his brothers. At his school in London, the students laughed at the way he spoke. But Fleming was bright and loved games and quickly made friends.

a British Army camp in England

In 1900, Fleming and his brothers joined the army.
While in the army, Fleming found he was good at sports.
He won awards for rifle-shooting,
he learned to swim and he joined a water polo team.

Love of Sports

Fleming's love of sports played a part in what he wanted to do with his life. In 1901, he decided to become a doctor at St Mary's Hospital.
He chose to study at St Mary's because it had a water polo team!

Fleming's laboratory at St Mary's Hospital

Running Words 206

Fleming in his laboratory

By 1905, Fleming had nearly finished his studies,
and he needed a job.
He wanted to stay at St Mary's because it had
a rifle-shooting team,
and Fleming was the best in the team!
St Mary's didn't want to lose him to another hospital,
so they gave him a job in the Inoculation Department.

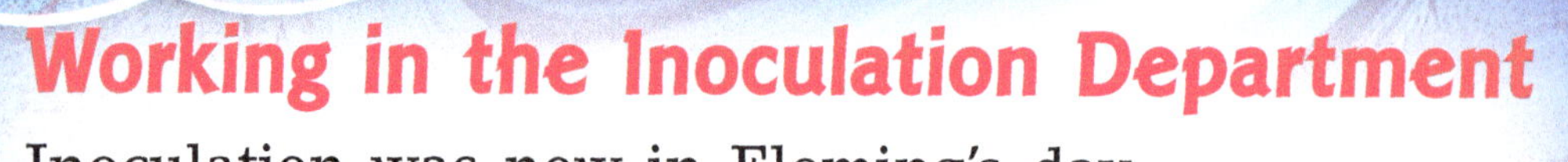

Working in the Inoculation Department

Inoculation was new in Fleming's day, and doctors were excited about it.

Inoculation stops people from getting a disease. Doctors inject people with a weaker form of the bacteria that causes the disease.

men being inoculated against typhoid

Fleming in his laboratory at St Mary's

Fleming's job was to collect bacteria from sick people in the hospital. Then, he had to look at the bacteria under a microscope in his laboratory.

Chapter 3

THE FIRST WORLD WAR

The **First World War** began in 1914.
During the war, Fleming went to work in a hospital in France.
There, he saw that many soldiers died
not from their wounds,
but from infections in their wounds.

injured soldiers

This made Fleming determined to find a way to help the body fight infections. After the end of the war in 1918, Fleming returned to St Mary's Hospital to carry on his work on bacteria.

Chapter 4

A PUZZLING DISCOVERY

In September 1928, Fleming left some glass dishes, on a bench in his laboratory for two weeks. When he came back, he noticed something puzzling.

Bacteria was growing on all the glass dishes except for one. On this dish mould had started to grow – the kind found on old bread.

mouldy bread

mould growing on Fleming's glass dish

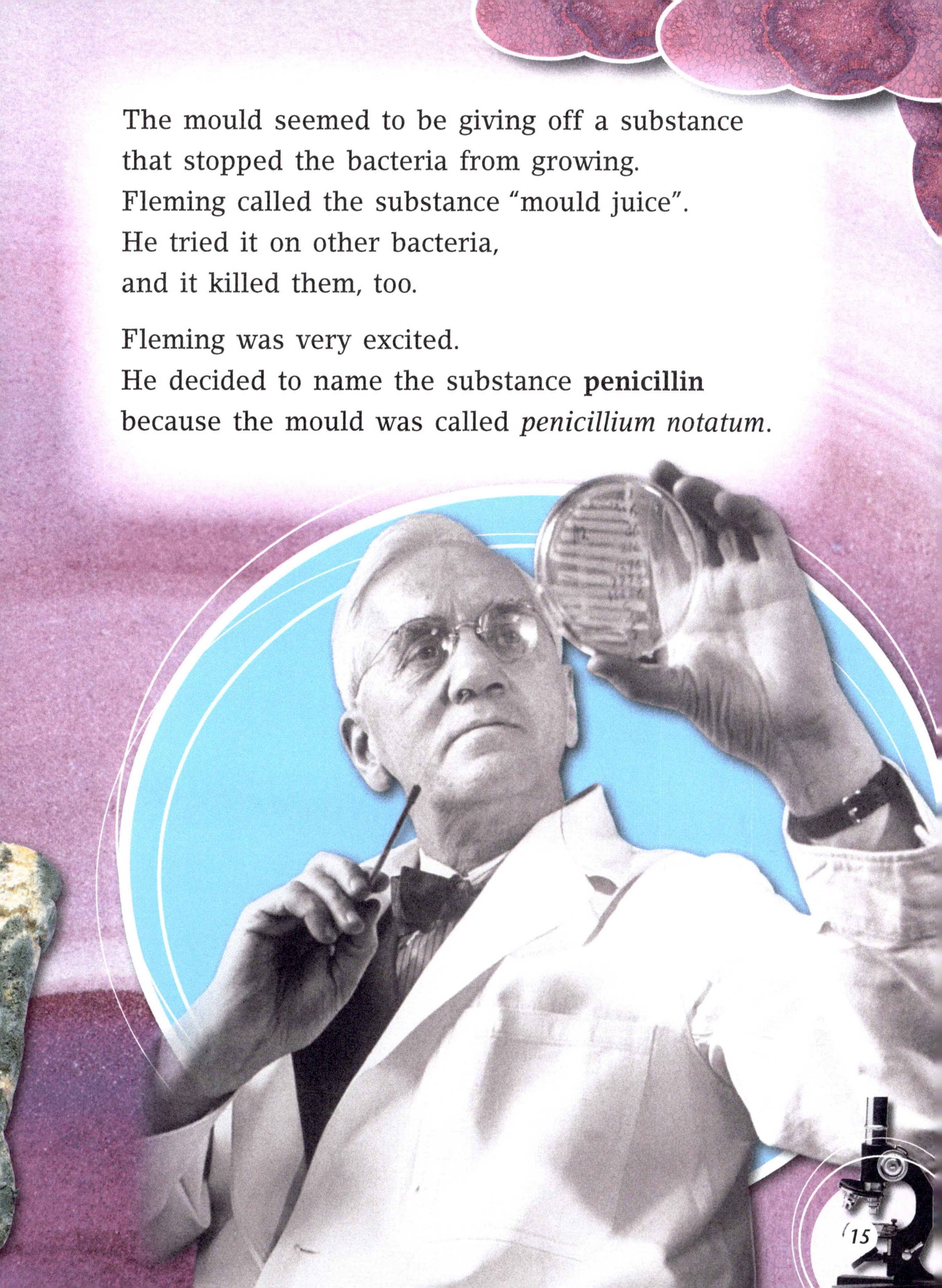

The mould seemed to be giving off a substance that stopped the bacteria from growing. Fleming called the substance "mould juice". He tried it on other bacteria, and it killed them, too.

Fleming was very excited. He decided to name the substance **penicillin** because the mould was called *penicillium notatum*.

Fleming tried to get his boss at St Mary's interested in penicillin.
Unfortunately, Fleming's boss thought he was wasting his time.
Like many doctors at that time,
Fleming's boss thought finding a way to kill bacteria was impossible.

Fleming did a few more experiments with penicillin, and he also wrote about it so other scientists could learn about it.
But, because no one seemed interested in his discovery, he forgot about penicillin and started to work on other things.

Chapter 5

THE WORK OF CHAIN AND FLOREY

In 1939, Ernst Chain, a scientist, discovered Fleming's notes. Chain and his boss, Howard Florey, were looking for medicines that could kill bacteria. They decided to test penicillin.

Ernst Chain

Howard Florey

But, Florey's team found it hard to grow enough penicillin for their tests.
They tried growing it in different kinds of trays, boxes and even bottles, but it grew very slowly.
Then, one day, they tried growing it in a hospital bedpan.
It worked and the mould began to grow.

In May 1940, Chain and Florey decided to experiment with penicillin. They gave penicillin to some sick mice, while they didn't give penicillin to some other sick mice. The mice that were given penicillin survived, but the ones that didn't get penicillin died. Florey declared: "It looks like a miracle!"

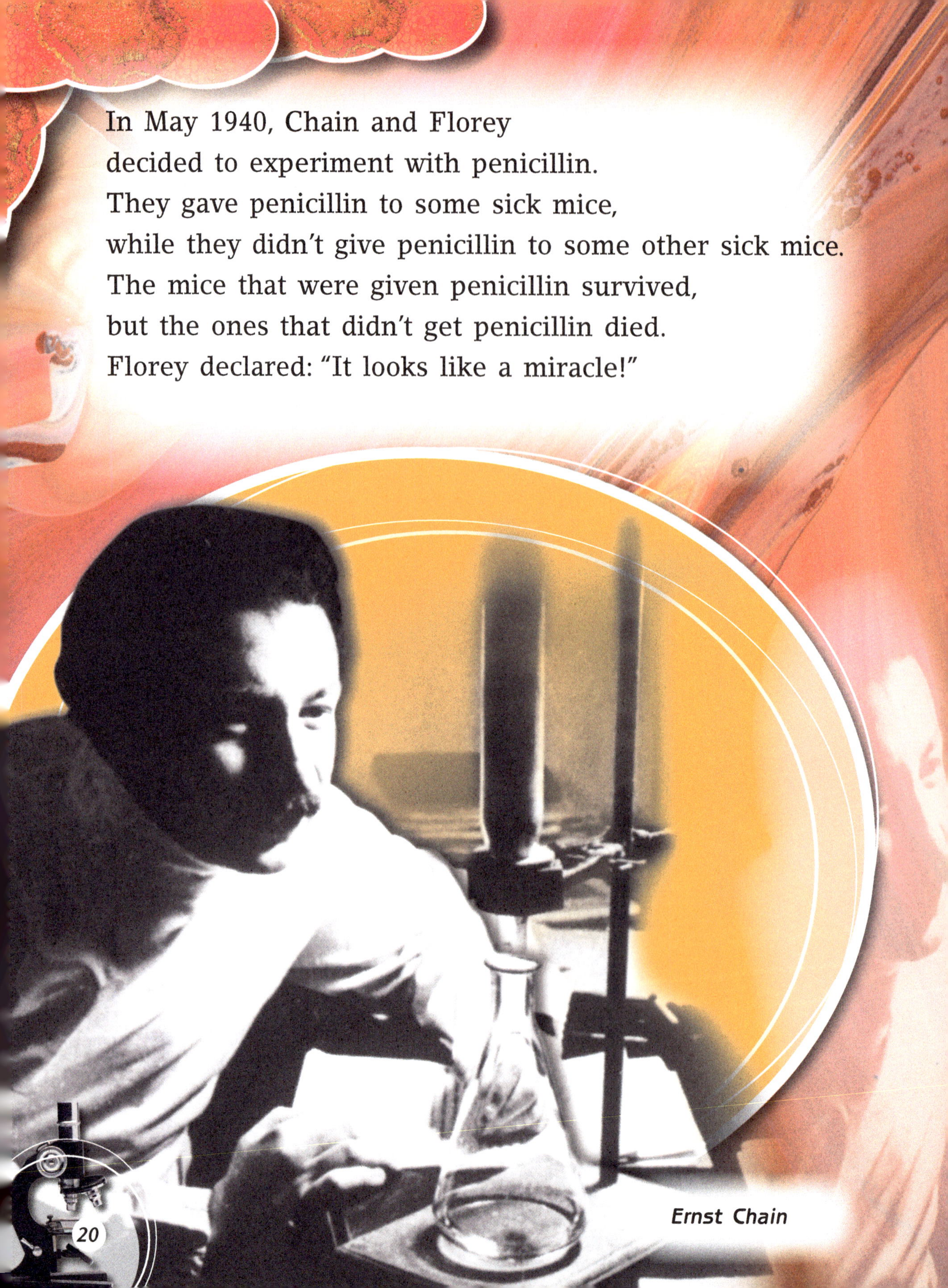

Ernst Chain

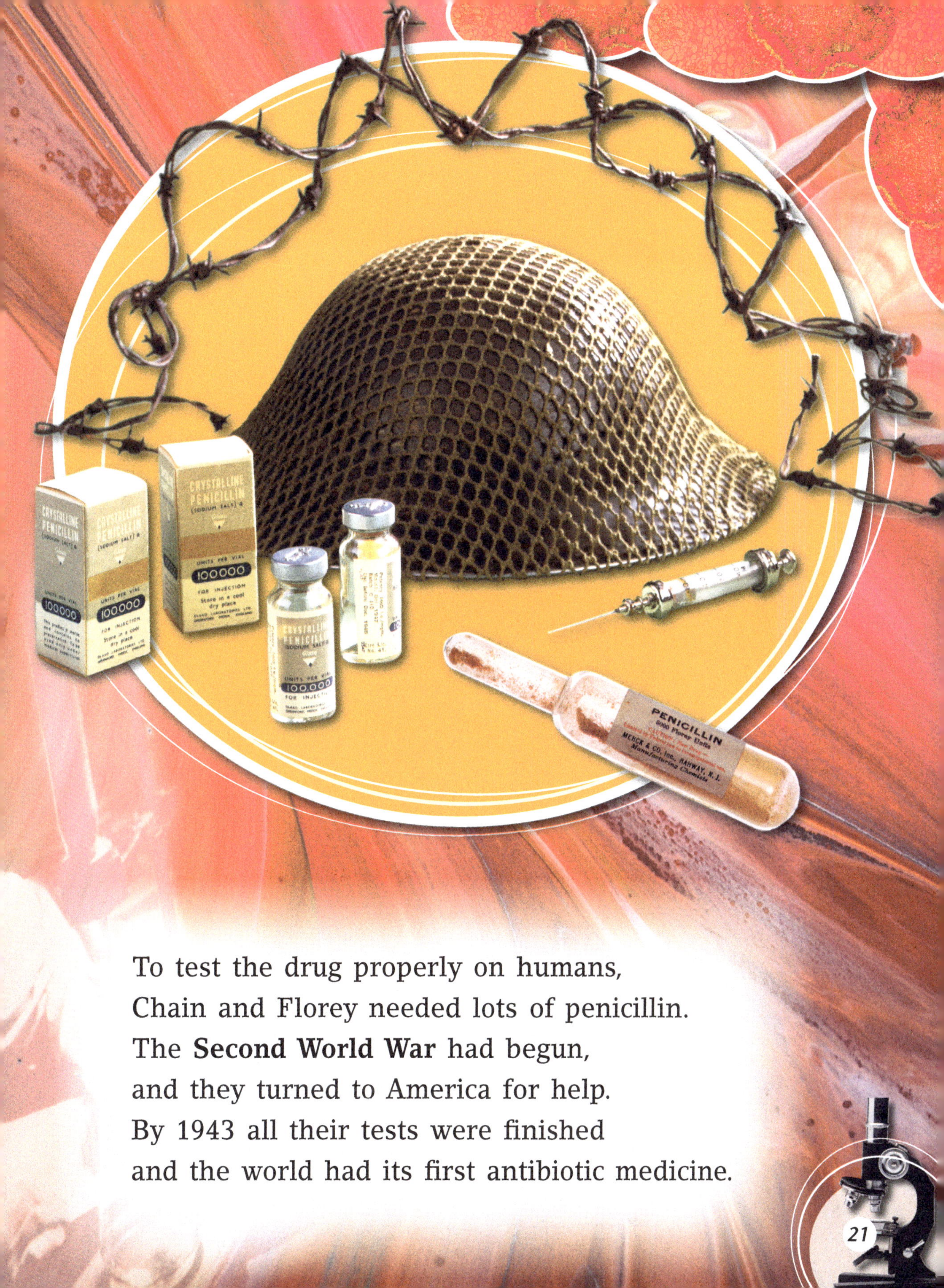

To test the drug properly on humans,
Chain and Florey needed lots of penicillin.
The **Second World War** had begun,
and they turned to America for help.
By 1943 all their tests were finished
and the world had its first antibiotic medicine.

Chapter 6

CONCLUSION

Fleming received many awards for his work in discovering penicillin.
He was proud of what he had done, but he always praised Chain and Florey for their work, too.
In 1945, they all shared the **Nobel Prize** for their important work.

Nobel Prize winners, 1945

At the age of 73, Fleming became very sick with pneumonia.
Thanks to penicillin, he survived.
Fleming died in 1955 and was buried in St Paul's Cathedral, alongside other great British heroes.

Glossary

bacteria	single cell micro-organisms. Many bacteria cause diseases and infections.
cells	the structural and functional units of all living things. Cells are called the 'building blocks of life'.
First World War	a world war fought between 1914 and 1918
infections	bacteria that has spread and multiplied causing sickness or death
Nobel Prize	an international prize awarded annually for outstanding work in chemistry, physics, literature, peace, physiology or medicine, and economics
penicillin	an antibiotic produced naturally by certain moulds and used in the treatment of bacterial infections
Second World War	a world war fought between 1939 and 1945
typhoid	a bacterial infection causing fever, red spots on the chest and abdomen, and severe intestinal pain. If left untreated, typhoid can cause death.

Index